Animal
Crosswords

Phil Clarke

Illustrated by the Pope Twins

Designed by Michael Hill

How to solve crosswords

The crosswords in this book start simple and gradually get harder. If you're new to crosswords, here are a few tips.

It's a good idea to use a pencil with an eraser or to write lightly with a pen so that you can remove or write over mistakes.

There are two lists of clues: one for answers that read across the crossword grid, and one for those that read down. Some answers have both an across and a down part.

Start wherever you like. If you can't solve one clue, move onto another that crosses it. The letters from that answer will help you. For example, solving the down answers below gives you B_R_S for 4 across, leading you towards the answer: BIRDS

ACROSS

1. Mash food with your teeth (4)
4. Feathered flying animals (5)
5. Job, errand (4)

DOWN

2. Hard, pointed growths on some animals' heads (5)
3. Past tense of "is" (3)
4. Bacon, lettuce and tomato sandwich (1.1.1.)

	¹C	²H	E	³W
		O		A
⁴B		R		S
L		N		
⁵T	A	S	K	

After each clue you can see how many letters the answer has, and whether it contains one word or more.

If you get stuck, or your answers don't seem to fit, you can check all the answers at the back of the book.

Happy puzzling!

ACROSS

1. A snail's protective case (5)
4. Red-breasted bird (5)
5. A dog's feet (4)

DOWN

1. Flat, narrow piece of something (5)
2. Arm joint (5)
3. Dry ground (4)

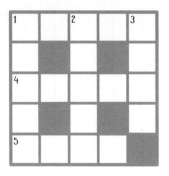

ACROSS

1. Talon (4)
4. Japanese rice rolls (5)
5. A bird's mouth (4)

DOWN

1. Price (4)
2. Passage between supermarket shelves (5)
3. Very pale red (4)

3

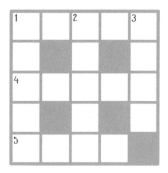

ACROSS

1. Young hero of *The Lion King* (5)
4. The lion in the Narnia stories (5)
5. Opposite of west (4)

DOWN

1. The largest portion is known as "the lion's _ _ _ _ _" (5)
2. Becomes liquid (5)
3. Zits (4)

4

ACROSS

1. Zodiac sign of the Lion (3)
4. Group of lions (5)
5. You catch fish in one (3)

DOWN

1. You use these to kiss (4)
2. Vegetable that can make you cry (5)
3. What carnivores eat (4)

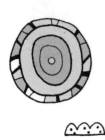

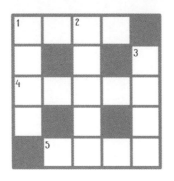

ACROSS

1. The sound a lion makes (4)
4. Rove around in search of prey (5)
5. Lazy (4)

DOWN

1. Tears (4)
2. At a high enough volume to be heard (5)
3. Hint (4)

6

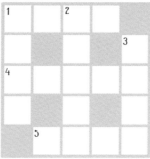

ACROSS

1. A bee colony lives in this (4)
4. Opposite of winner (5)
5. Striped flying insect (4)

DOWN

1. Opening, cavity (4)
2. Wide-open view (5)
3. Outing (4)

7

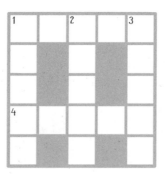

ACROSS

1. Big bee that is mother to most of a colony (5)
4. Wasps and bees can do this to defend themselves (5)

DOWN

1. Heroic mission (5)
2. The King of Rock and Roll (5)
3. Poke gently (5)

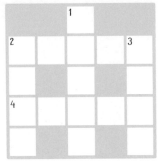

8

ACROSS

2. Male bee (5)

4. If something is "the bee's _ _ _ _ _"
it is really good (5)

DOWN

1. Sweet food made by bees (5)

2. Noble rank below prince (4)

3. Simple (4)

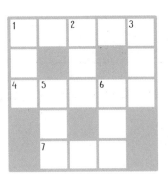

9

ACROSS

1. Large cloud of flying insects (5)

4. Put your clothes on (5)

7. Substance from which bees
make honeycomb (3)

DOWN

1. Unhappy (3)

2. Playing card (3)

3. Title for a married woman (3)

5. Uncooked (3)

6. How many legs do
insects have? (3)

10

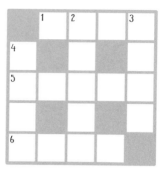

ACROSS

1. Wealthy (4)
5. A cow's milk comes out of this (5)
6. Dutch cheese covered in red wax (4)

DOWN

2. South Asian country (5)
3. Group of cows (4)
4. Summer month (4)

11

ACROSS

1. Aberdeen _ _ _ _ _, black cattle breed (5)
4. A reckless person may be said to act "like a bull in a _ _ _ _ _ shop" (5)
5. Cattle meat (4)

DOWN

1. Curved roof support (4)
2. Move smoothly and quickly (5)
3. It keeps your neck warm (5)

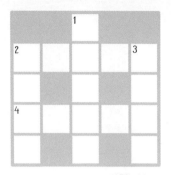

12

ACROSS

2. Loop of rope used by cowboys to catch cattle (5)
4. Feed on grass (5)

DOWN

1. Typical (5)
2. Sawn-off pieces of tree (4)
3. Strong cattle used for heavy work (4)

13

ACROSS

1. Male cow (4)
3. Place where cows are milked, or their milk is bottled (5)
5. Long periods of time (4)

DOWN

1. You sleep on this (3)
2. Fibbing (5)
4. Opposite of no (3)

14

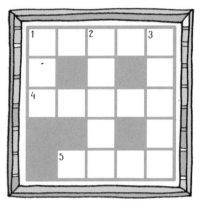

ACROSS

1. Cat with a patterned coat (5)
4. Sulky (5)
5. "My Gran always _ _ _ _ her old socks as dusters" (4)

DOWN

1. Male cat (3)
2. Puss-in-_ _ _ _ _, talking fairy-tale cat (5)
3. Toys that go up and down on strings (2-3)

15

ACROSS

1. Cats are said to have nine of these (5)
4. *Hello* _ _ _ _ _, Japanese cartoon cat (5)
5. Toy you can dress up (4)

DOWN

1. Enjoyed (5)
2. Essential (5)
3. Speaks (4)

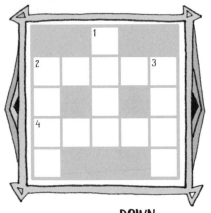

ACROSS

2. Dr. _ _ _ _ _ wrote
   The Cat in the Hat (5)
4. It's fired with a bow (5)

DOWN

1. The sound of a contented cat (4)
2. Celebrity (4)
3. Uses a needle and thread (4)

17

ACROSS

1. Tempest (5)
4. Person on a horse's back (5)
5. Small type of horse (4)

DOWN

1. Leather strip for fastening (5)
2. "In the _ _ _ _ _ days" means a long time ago (5)
3. Female horse (4)

18

ACROSS

1. Certain (4)
3. Fast (5)
4. Two _ _ _ _ two is four (4)

DOWN

1. A horse's own compartment in a stable (5)
2. These are used to control a horse (5)

ACROSS

3. Climb onto a horse (5)
4. Some people think horseshoes are _ _ _ _ _ charms (5)

DOWN

1. Speedy (5)
2. Stopover, break (4)
3. A cross between a donkey and a horse (4)

20

ACROSS

1. The hair on a horse's head (4)
4. Large horse bred for heavy work (5)
5. Head cook (4)

DOWN

1. Face disguise (4)
2. The sound a horse makes (5)
3. Part of a plant (4)

21

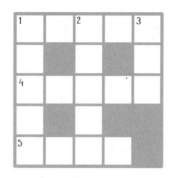

ACROSS

1. Hairy wild pigs (5)
4. European country famous for pasta and pizza (5)
5. Hold on to (4)

DOWN

1. In *The Three Little Pigs*, the house that the Big Bad Wolf couldn't blow down was built of this (5)
2. Opposite of asleep (5)
3. Pig pen (3)

22

ACROSS

1. Cartoon pig with a brother named George (5)
4. Waste metal (5)
5. What "big" and "pig" do (5)

DOWN

1. Show-off (5)
2. Celebration (5)
3. Fruit (5)

23

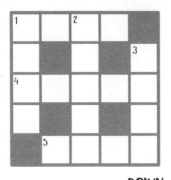

ACROSS

1. Movie based on the novel *The Sheep-Pig* (4)
4. Another word for pigs (5)
5. Stair (4)

DOWN

1. Sunbathe (4)
2. Constructed (5)
3. Assist (4)

24

ACROSS

1. Pig (3)
4. Pig's nose (5)
5. Female pig (3)

DOWN

1. Quiet (4)
2. Gets bigger (5)
3. Dish slowly cooked in gravy (4)

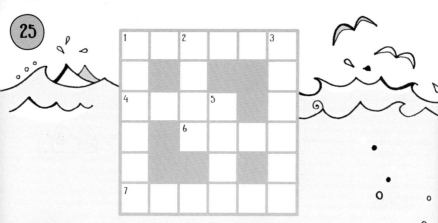

25

ACROSS

1. A sea _ _ _ _ _ _ is a spiny ocean creature (6)
4. What you aim at in soccer (4)
6. The part of you that thinks (4)
7. Shelled sea reptile (6)

DOWN

1. Important, pressing (6)
2. Shellfish (4)
3. Sewing tool (6)
5. Raise (4)

26

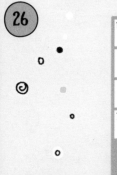
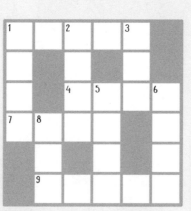

ACROSS

1. A _ _ _ _ _ reef is a rocky, undersea structure full of plant-like animals (5)
4. Three goes _ _ _ _ six twice (4)
7. Part of a skeleton (4)
9. People with no common sense (5)

DOWN

1. Clawed sea creature (4)
2. Wreck (4)
3. Allow (3)
5. *Finding* _ _ _ _ Disney movie about a lost clownfish (4)
6. Rowing-poles (4)
8. Opposite of on (3)

ACROSS

1. Soft, holey sea creature (6)
4. Wander (4)
6. Ooze (4)
7. Precious stones sometimes found in oysters (6)

DOWN

1. Small, lobster-like sea creatures (6)
2. Title (4)
3. Explodes like a volcano (6)
5. The largest continent (4)

28

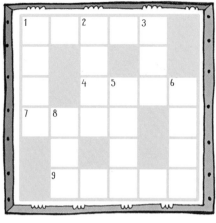

ACROSS

1. _ _ _ _ _ dogs help disabled owners get around (5)
4. Follow commands (4)
7. The Great _ _ _ _ is a very big breed of dog (4)
9. Underground worker (5)

DOWN

1. Opposite of bad (4)
2. Metal (4)
3. Organ of sight (3)
5. Vegetable (4)
6. Each has 12 months (4)
8. Upper limb (3)

Westie

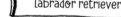

labrador retriever

Dachshund

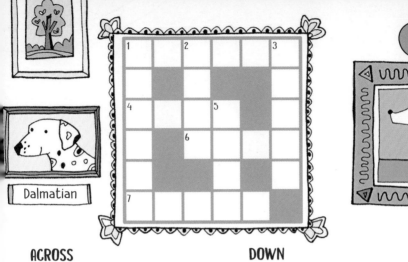

Dalmatian

ACROSS

1. Short-legged breed of hound (6)
4. Back of the foot (4)
6. Change position (4)
7. Wild Australian dog (5)

DOWN

1. To the rear (6)
2. Appear, look (4)
3. Robber (5)
5. Opposite of short (4)

German Shepherd

ACROSS

1. "You can't teach an old dog new _ _ _ _ _ _." (6)
4. This word means "to do with dogs" (6)
5. Masters, nobles (5)

DOWN

1. Try to make someone laugh by touching them lightly (6)
2. Pay no attention to (6)
3. Types (5)

31

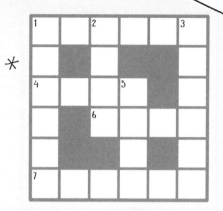

ACROSS

1. Underground animal home (6)
4. Moist (4)
6. You hear with them (4)
7. Uncover, show (6)

DOWN

1. Sturdy animal with a black-and-white face (6)
2. Capital of Italy (4)
3. "Pop! goes the _ _ _ _ _ _" (6)
5. Light, faint (4)

32

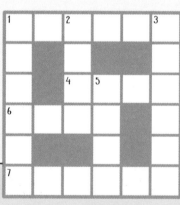

ACROSS

1. Animal in the weasel family (6)
4. Requests (4)
6. Small burrowing animal with a velvety, black coat (4)
7. Shake noisily (6)

DOWN

1. One who works the land (6)
2. Genuine (4)
3. Paper handkerchief (6)
5. Chair (4)

ACROSS

1. Small, mouse-like animal with a long, pointed snout (5)
4. Fail to hit (4)
6. In this place (4)
8. Work dough with your hands (5)

DOWN

1. Slide over snow on long runners (3)
2. Sweet-smelling flower (4)
3. Payment for work done (4)
4. Humble, timid (4)
5. Item of footwear (4)
7. Pole (3)

34

ACROSS

1. Disney cartoon mouse (6)
4. Large rodents (4)
7. "and they all lived happily _ _ _ _ after" (4)
9. _ _ _ _ _ _ *Little*, movie about a talking mouse (6)

DOWN

1. Labyrinth (4)
2. Middle of an apple (4)
3. Consume (3)
5. Space (4)
6. Common condiment (4)
8. Animal doctor (3)

35

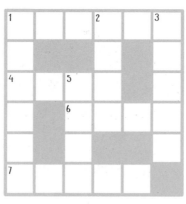

ACROSS

1. Mice are often seen eating this in cartoons (6)
4. Sad or weary sound (4)
6. Short message (4)
7. Opposite of higher (5)

DOWN

1. Informal, relaxed (6)
2. Sound that repeats and fades (4)
3. Artist's painting stand (5)
5. Nibble or chew something (4)

ACROSS

1. "Hickory, dickory, dock, the mouse ran up the _ _ _ _ _" (5)
4. Long, epic stories (5)
6. Cartoon mouse chased by Tom the cat (5)
7. "Three _ _ _ _ _ mice, see how they run" (5)

DOWN

2. Deceiver (4)
3. Sticky mud (4)
4. Make airtight or watertight (4)
5. Broad smile (4)

ACROSS

1. Fail to remember (6)
4. Old-fashioned word for "you" (4)
6. An oak, for example (4)
7. Dignified, principled (5)

DOWN

1. Tie up, secure (6)
2. Pace, speed (4)
3. An elephant's long nose (5)
5. Cure (4)

ACROSS

1. _ _ _ _ _ _ elephants have smaller ears than their African cousins (6)
5. Amaze, knock out (4)
7. Mix with a spoon (4)
9. An elephant's two huge teeth (5)

DOWN

2. Tree fruit with a hard shell (3)
3. Short for "is not" (4)
4. Close by (4)
5. Injection (4)
6. Purposes (4)
8. Belonging to it (3)

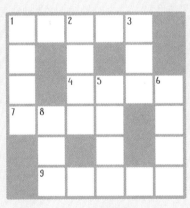

ACROSS

1. Name of a famous elephant now used as a word for "very big" (5)
4. Uses a chair (4)
7. Final (4)
9. Disney's flying elephant (5)

DOWN

1. Prison (4)
2. This simple green plant grows on rocks (4)
3. Opposite of in (3)
5. Thing in a list (4)
6. Harrison Ford played Han _ _ _ _ (4)
8. As well as (3)

ACROSS

1. Move on foot (4)
4. Tavern (3)
5. This African flightless bird is the largest bird in the world (7)
8. Big, flightless bird from Australia (3)
9. Many deserts are covered in it (4)

DOWN

1. Hairpieces (4)
2. Flightless bird from New Zealand (4)
3. Measurement equal to about 2.5cm (4)
5. Opposite of shut (4)
6. In this way (4)
7. You might send one with a birthday greeting (4)

ACROSS

1. Flightless birds famous for dying out (5)
4. Tall, yellow character on *Sesame Street* (3, 4)
6. Particular, different (7)
7. Dripping wet (5)

DOWN

1. Payments that are owed (5)
2. Earth-moving machines (7)
3. Grinning (7)
5. Pause, interruption (5)

ACROSS

1. Leader of the wolf pack in *The Jungle Book*, often used as a name for Scout leaders (5)
4. Young wolf (3)
6. _ _ _ _ _ *and the Wolf*, Russian musical fairy tale (5)
7. _ _ _ _ _ Hood, legendary outlaw (5)
8. Short for avenue (3)
9. Language of the Netherlands (5)

DOWN

1. Tame, llama-like animal (6)
2. Went inside (7)
3. Gymnast, tumbler (7)
5. Part of a tree (6)

ACROSS

3. Precious metal (6)
4. A wolf's home (3)
5. *The ___ Who Cried "Wolf"* is a story with the moral "Don't tell lies" (3)
7. Little Red _____ Hood met a wolf disguised as her grandmother (6)

DOWN

1. Sick (3)
2. Be part of (6)
3. Picturesque (6)
6. Strike (3)

44

ACROSS

1. If you've done this to your toe, you've banged it painfully against something (7)
5. Tree-climbing North American animal with black markings like an eye-mask (7)
7. Startled (7)
9. Big, hairy, ice age elephant (7)

DOWN

2. Drink made from leaves (3)
3. Flower (5)
4. Sat down for a meal (5)
5. Kingdom (5)
6. Appeal, attractiveness (5)
8. Devour (3)

ACROSS

1. Striped North American animal known for its smelly spray (5)
4. Another name for American bison (7)
6. The world's most widely-spoken language (7)
7. Very tall building or structure (5)

DOWN

1. Wept loudly (6)
2. Drab shade of light brown used for military uniforms (5)
3. North American burrowing rodent that digs tunnel networks (6)
5. Squabble (5)

46

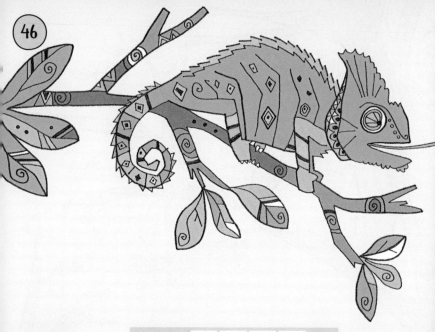

ACROSS

1. Poke (4)
5. Show, exhibit (7)
6. Computer screen, or a large lizard (7)
7. Plant stalk (4)

DOWN

2. Type of scaly creature, such as a snake or turtle (7)
3. Komodo _ _ _ _ _ _, the world's largest lizard (6)
4. Plane drivers (6)

ACROSS

1. Large lizards with spiny crests, sometimes kept as pets (7)
5. More frightening (7)
7. Chameleons catch insects with their long, sticky _ _ _ _ _ _ _ (7)
8. Order somebody what to do (7)

DOWN

2. Wall-climbing tropical lizard (5)
3. Okay (7)
4. Polite title for a man you don't know (3)
6. Occasion (5)
7. Smidgen (3)

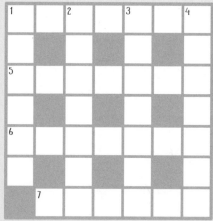

ACROSS

1. Little red insect with a burning bite (4, 3)
5. More delicious (7)
6. Capital of Kenya (7)
7. Get away (6)

DOWN

1. _ _ _ _ _ _ ants travel through the air in summer to start a new colony (6)
2. Stays (7)
3. In which US state is the Grand Canyon? (7)
4. Insect that lives in large groups and may build enormous mounds (7)

ACROSS

1. _____ ants are tiny, yellow insects that share their name with the rulers of Ancient Egypt (7)
4. Baby's bedroom (7)
7. Type of ant that fights to protect the colony (7)
9. Spectacles (7)

DOWN

1. If someone is fidgety, you might say they have "ants in their _____" (5)
2. The fourth month (5)
3. Belonging to us (3)
5. Ways out (5)
6. There are 1,760 in a mile (5)
8. Slippery substance (3)

50

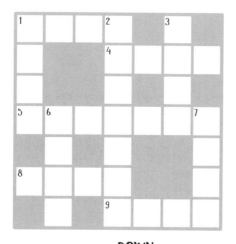

ACROSS

1. (with 1 down) Giant movie ape who climbed the Empire State Building (4, 4)
4. Fairy-tale monster (4)
5. Giant slain by David in the Bible (7)
8. The main difference between an ape and a monkey is that an ape has no _ _ _ _ (4)
9. Equipped, ready (4)

DOWN

1. (see 1 across)
2. The world's largest ape (7)
3. Spoiled child (4)
6. Egg-shaped (4)
7. Enormous (4)

ACROSS

1. Floating spheres of gas (7)
5. These apes are amazing swingers and singers (7)
6. The time that followed the Bronze Age (4, 3)
7. Dwell (6)

DOWN

1. Looser-fitting (7)
2. Large monkeys with long, dog-like muzzles (7)
3. _____ Nimoy played Mr. Spock in Star Trek (7)
4. Your parents' daughter (6)

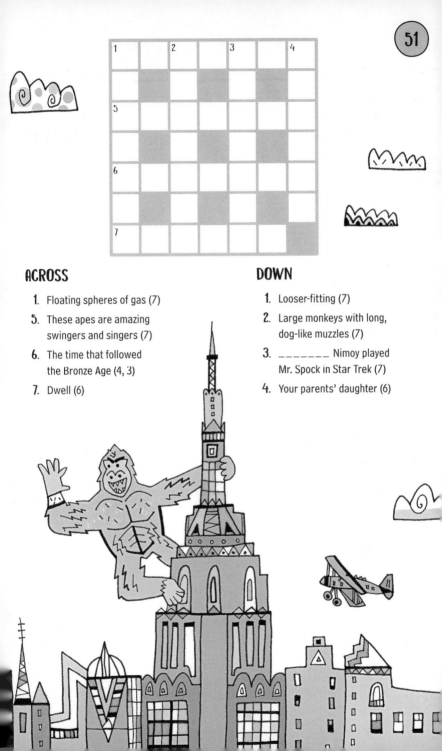

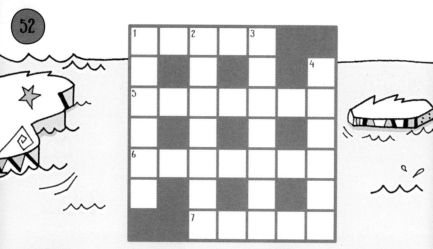

ACROSS

1. Amy _ _ _ _ _ starred in *Enchanted* and played Lois Lane in *Man of Steel* (5)
5. North American reindeer (7)
6. Big lump of frozen seawater (7)
7. _ _ _ _ _ owls are white birds of prey that live in the Far North (5)

DOWN

1. Area around the North Pole (6)
2. Stuffy (7)
3. Colder than freezing (3-4)
4. Famished (6)

ACROSS

1. Another name for killer whales (5)
4. Pull another vehicle with yours (3)
6. _ _ _ _ _ bears live in the Arctic (5)
7. Opposite of outer (5)
8. French for "water" (3)
9. Searches for (5)

DOWN

1. Resist, stand against (6)
2. Anders _ _ _ _ _ _ _ was a Swedish scientist who invented a famous temperature scale (7)
3. Weird (7)
5. Big, fat, seal-like animal with enormous tusks (6)

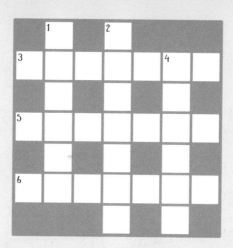

ACROSS

3. Grasshoppers that swarm in vast numbers and can destroy crops (7)
5. Earthenware, ceramics (7)
6. Desert animal famed for standing upright on guard duty (7)

DOWN

1. Wolf-like wild dog of the North American deserts (6)
2. Large desert bird that feeds on dead animals (7)
4. Danger (6)

ACROSS

1. Humped desert animal (5)
4. You breathe it (3)
6. Wailing warning signal (5)
7. Lime and olive are shades of this (5)
8. The opposite of "Nay" (3)
9. Spanish for Mister (5)

DOWN

1. The world's largest inland sea, it shares its name with a prince in C.S. Lewis's Narnia books (7)
2. Illusions seen in hot places, often of water that is not really there (7)
3. Lamp (7)
5. The Road _____ is a speedy desert bird hunted in vain by Wile E. Coyote (6)

ACROSS

1. Spaces in between (4)
4. Spotted African big cat (7)
6. A black _ _ _ _ _ _ _ is a rare 4 across with dark fur (7)
7. Fight, box (4)

DOWN

1. Adult (5-2)
2. Illegal animal hunter (7)
3. Lose your footing on a wet surface (4)
5. Shoot forward suddenly (4)

ACROSS

4. North American wildcat also known as the red lynx (6)

6. These are the biggest cats in South America (7)

7. Job, occupation (6)

DOWN

1. Another name for pumas or mountain lions (7)

2. Scratched, scoured (7)

3. Secret supply (5)

5. Fire out with force (5)

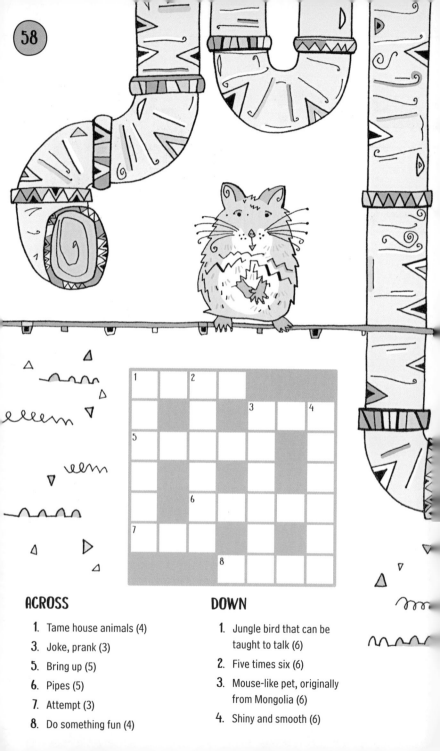

ACROSS

1. Tame house animals (4)
3. Joke, prank (3)
5. Bring up (5)
6. Pipes (5)
7. Attempt (3)
8. Do something fun (4)

DOWN

1. Jungle bird that can be taught to talk (6)
2. Five times six (6)
3. Mouse-like pet, originally from Mongolia (6)
4. Shiny and smooth (6)

ACROSS

1. From which Middle Eastern country did the 5 across originally come? (5)
5. The golden _ _ _ _ _ _ _ is a tubby rodent often kept as a pet. It can store a lot of food in its cheeks. (7)
7. Girl's name (7)
10. Feeding dishes (5)

DOWN

1. The world's biggest desert (6)
2. Edge, lip (3)
3. Perform in a play (3)
4. Pieces of food given to reward a pet (6)
6. Short for Susan (3)
8. It protects a baby's clothes at mealtimes (3)
9. Farm animal (3)

ACROSS

1. Giant grass eaten by giant pandas (6)
4. _ _ _ _ _ _-the-Pooh, famous bear (6)
6. Pulse, rhythm (4)
7. Stumble (4)
8. They are black or green and often sprinkled on pizza (6)
9. Kind, not harsh (6)

DOWN

1. Yogi Bear's little pal (3-3)
2. What you put on a fish-hook (4)
3. Possessors, keepers (6)
4. Coming out of sleep (6)
5. The _ _ _ _ _ _ Strikes Back, Star Wars movie (6)
7. Young person aged 13–19 (4)

ACROSS

1. ____-__ *Panda*, movie about Po, a bear who masters the martial arts (4-2)
5. Make clearer (7)
7. Verse (4)
9. Observes (4)
12. Big North American brown bear (7)
13. Shooting star (6)

DOWN

1. Strikes with the foot (5)
2. Tidier (6)
3. Toss (4)
4. Stain, pigment (3)
6. Comic bear on *The Muppet Show* (6)
8. Town leader (5)
10. Protective shell for a baby bird (3)
11. Extent, dimensions (4)

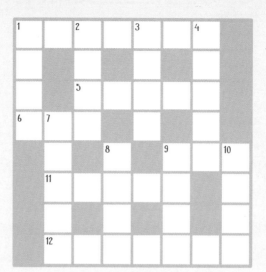

ACROSS

1. The fastest of all big cats (7)
5. Serpent (5)
6. Plural of "is" (3)
9. Nickname for an Apple Computer (3)
11. Striped African horse relative (5)
12. Flower-shaped award badge (7)

DOWN

1. Coke or Pepsi (4)
2. Comfort (4)
3. Sporting side (4)
4. "Laughing" African predator (5)
7. Shaving tool (5)
8. Wading bird with a long, curved beak (4)
9. Sail-pole (4)
10. _ _ _ _ Town is a big city in South Africa (4)

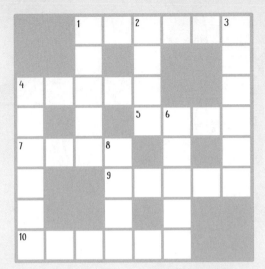

ACROSS

1. African wildlife sightseeing trip (6)
4. Gem (5)
5. List of meal choices (4)
7. Secret writing (4)
9. What's the name of the zebra in the *Madagascar* movies? (5)
10. Someone who represents you in court (6)

DOWN

1. Planted seeds in the ground (5)
2. Movie (4)
3. A broken arm, for example (6)
4. Wild dog found in Africa and Asia (6)
6. Mistake (5)
8. TV equivalent of an Oscar (4)

64

ACROSS

1. Large, hopping Australian animal (8)
5. Heavenly messenger (5)
6. Mount _ _ _ _, Italian volcano (4)
9. Deeds (4)
12. Marsupials are animals that carry their young in a _ _ _ _ _ (5)
13. The duck-billed _ _ _ _ _ _ _ _ is an egg-laying mammal from Australia (8)

DOWN

1. Small, bear-like, tree-dwelling marsupial (5)
2. It follows day (5)
3. Shaft joining two wheels (4)
4. You use it for baking and roasting (4)
7. Donald J. _ _ _ _ _, US president (5)
8. Burnt remains (5)
10. Pleasantly cold (4)
11. Round mark (4)

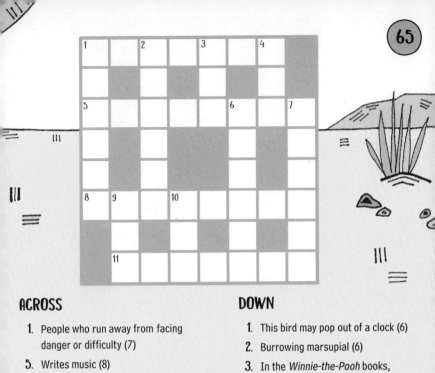

ACROSS

1. People who run away from facing danger or difficulty (7)
5. Writes music (8)
8. Eye expert who give you sight tests (8)
11. Small relative of the kangaroo (7)

DOWN

1. This bird may pop out of a clock (6)
2. Burrowing marsupial (6)
3. In the *Winnie-the-Pooh* books, Kanga's little son (3)
4. Take someone to court, asking that they be made to pay you (3)
6. Spit (6)
7. Australia's biggest city (6)
9. Long church bench (3)
10. Short for I will (3)

66

ACROSS

1. Large hawk common in Europe and Asia (7)
5. Alright (2)
7. Fish-eating bird of prey also known as the sea hawk (6)
9. These divide tennis courts (4)
10. A plant grows from it (4)
12. US currency (6)
13. Mother (2)
15. Shocking news story (7)

DOWN

1. Bloom (7)
2. _ _ _ _ _ _-up means fastened (6)
3. Word ending a prayer (4)
4. Carry out, execute (2)
6. Hovering bird of prey (7)
8. Shouted (6)
11. _ _ _ _ the Explorer, Mexican cartoon heroine (4)
14. "_ _ easy _ _ pie" (2)

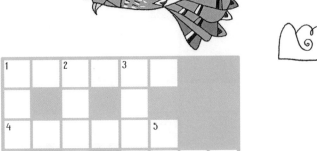

ACROSS

1. Huge South American vulture (6)
4. Bird of prey that shares its name with King Arthur's wizard (6)
6. Ripped (4)
8. Prepare a hot meal (4)
10. Electrics (6)
11. Harsh (6)

DOWN

1. Picture story magazine (5)
2. Thin (6)
3. Leave out, skip (4)
5. Sign (6)
7. The bald _ _ _ _ _ is America's national bird (5)
9. Bird of prey that shares its name with a wind-blown toy (4)

68

ACROSS

1. Asian snake with hood-like flaps around its head (5)
5. Unable to hear (4)
6. Large area of salt water (3)
7. The poison in a snake bite (5)
9. Step (5)
11. Help (3)
12. Conceal (4)
13. Answer (5)

DOWN

1. Expenses (5)
2. ___ constrictor, snake that kills by crushing (3)
3. Poisonous snake (5)
4. Glow around an angel's head (4)
7. Poisonous snake that bears live young (5)
8. Mucky, dirty (5)
10. Skinny (4)
11. Snake with a deadly bite (3)

ACROSS

2. The black _ _ _ _ _ is the fastest snake (5)
5. Ten divided by ten (3)
6. Capital of Ireland (6)
9. Heavy cold (3)
10. Long bread roll (3)
11. Detest (6)
14. To get _ _ _ of something is to dispose of it (3)
15. Long, pointed teeth (5)

DOWN

1. Merry (6)
2. In myth, she had snakes for hair (6)
3. Angry crowd (3)
4. Muhammad _ _ _, US boxer (3)
7. Powerful light beams (6)
8. No one (6)
12. Fool (3)
13. Heavy weight (3)

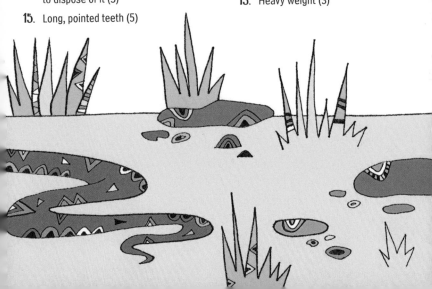

ACROSS

1. The world's tallest animal (7)
4. Irritates (6)
6. Break, division (4)
7. Get bigger (4)
8. Creatures from another planet (6)
9. Wild pig with a lumpy face, like Pumbaa in *The Lion King* (7)

DOWN

1. Female hippo in the *Madagascar* movies (6)
2. Slang for "am not" (4)
3. Levels of a building (6)
4. Which continent do hippos come from? (6)
5. Cutting wood (6)
7. Small, biting insect (4)

ACROSS

1. Dry grassland with scattered trees (8)
5. Less strong (6)
7. Positive answer (3)
9. ___ Baba and the Forty Thieves (3)
10. The reticulated _____ is the world's longest snake (6)
12. Perfectly clean (8)

DOWN

1. Be awake past your bedtime (4, 2)
2. Oaths (4)
3. Tidy (4)
4. A gorilla, for example (3)
6. Large African animals with horned noses (6)
8. Opposite of open (4)
9. ____ Boleyn, a wife of Henry VIII (4)
11. High-pitched bark (3)

ACROSS

1. Flat-bodied fish that can prick you painfully with its tail (8)
5. The only part of a shark you usually see above water is its ___ (3)
6. _____ rays are the largest fish of their kind (5)
8. Mechanical person (5)
10. Hole (3)
11. Animal that hunts other animals (8)

DOWN

1. More protected (5)
2. Lodge, roadhouse (3)
3. _____ white sharks are the biggest meat-eating fish (5)
4. Frequently (1, 3)
6. Large pile (5)
7. Following (5)
9. Above (4)
10. Jar (3)

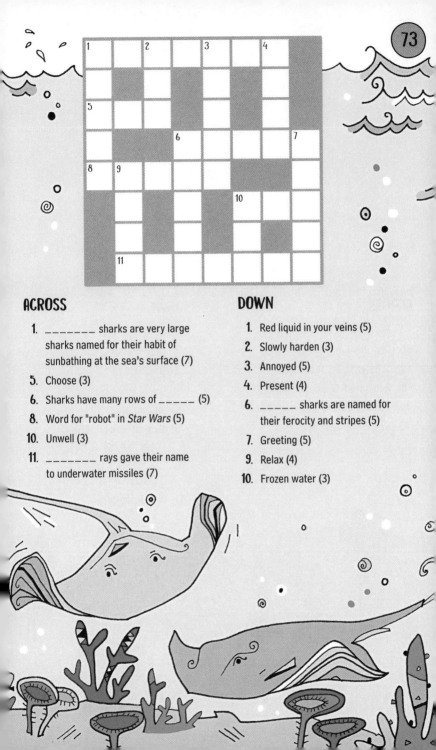

ACROSS

1. _ _ _ _ _ _ _ sharks are very large sharks named for their habit of sunbathing at the sea's surface (7)
5. Choose (3)
6. Sharks have many rows of _ _ _ _ _ (5)
8. Word for "robot" in *Star Wars* (5)
10. Unwell (3)
11. _ _ _ _ _ _ _ rays gave their name to underwater missiles (7)

DOWN

1. Red liquid in your veins (5)
2. Slowly harden (3)
3. Annoyed (5)
4. Present (4)
6. _ _ _ _ _ sharks are named for their ferocity and stripes (5)
7. Greeting (5)
9. Relax (4)
10. Frozen water (3)

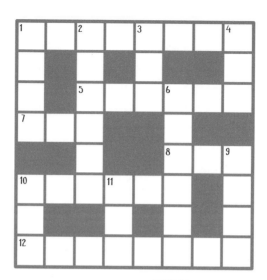

ACROSS

1. Bushy-tailed, tree-climbing rodent (8)

5. Plan, have in mind (6)

7. "I haven't ___ a clue!" (3)

8. Red-furred, dog-like animal (3)

10. Puzzling question (6)

12. By the shortest route (8)

DOWN

1. Adult male deer (4)

2. What the "U" in USA stands for (6)

3. Decay (3)

4. Boy or young man (3)

6. Result (6)

9. Medical scan that shows inside your body (1-3)

10. ___ deer are Europe's largest deer (3)

11. Female deer (3)

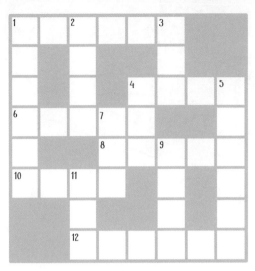

ACROSS

1. Oak nuts (6)

4. Fat, worm-like, baby insect (4)

6. Opposite of tight (5)

8. A wall made of bushes (5)

10. Red gemstone (4)

12. Number of months in a year (6)

DOWN

1. It grows on a deer's head (6)

2. Capital of Norway (4)

3. A knight's title (3)

4. "___-whiz!" (3)

5. Light wind (6)

7. Not confident (3)

9. Roald ____, author (4)

11. Gamble (3)

ACROSS

1. This bird can fan out its tail (7)
5. Biggest city in India, old name Bombay (6)
6. Opposite of "to" (4)
7. ____ cobras are the largest snakes of their kind (4)
8. Common black-and-white bird (6)
9. Rudyard _____ wrote *The Jungle Book* (7)

DOWN

1. Scent (7)
2. Pal (4)
3. Taxi driver (6)
4. Making a hole in the ground (7)
5. Young hero of *The Jungle Book* (6)
7. Execute (4)

ACROSS

1. _ _ _ _ _ _ _ _ tigers are huge big cats from the Russian Far East (8)
5. Map book (5)
6. Strikes with with a finger (4)
9. Coin-hole (4)
12. Wipe out, remove (5)
13. Group of words (8)

DOWN

1. Breaks suddenly (5)
2. In *The Jungle Book*, bear who helps Mowgli (5)
3. Orange-brown corroded metal (4)
4. As soon as possible (1.1.1.1.)
7. One more time (5)
8. _ _ _ _ _ Khan, ferocious tiger who is the villain of *The Jungle Book* (5)
10. Deep affection (4)
11. Typed message (4)

ACROSS

1. Huge seabird (9)
6. Something you play with (3)
7. Plump sea animals with flippers (5)
8. Garden tool (4)
10. The _ _ _ _ of Man is near Britain (4)
12. Two times (5)
13. Join numbers to make bigger ones (3)
14. Gigantic (8)

DOWN

1. Region around the South Pole (9)
2. Cove (3)
3. Experiment (4)
4. Rainbow gemstones (5)
5. Dangles (8)
9. Tiny, shrimp-like sea creatures (5)
11. You use them for hanging clothes (4)
13. Cry of discovery (3)

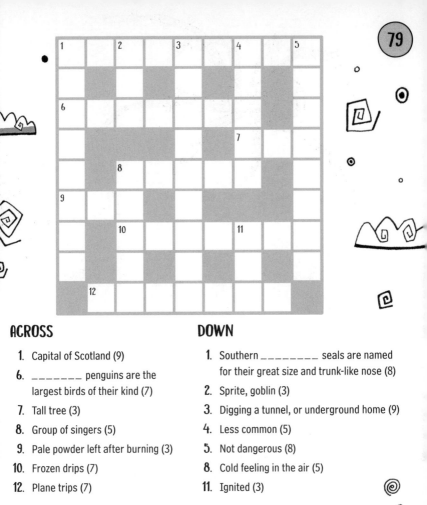

ACROSS

1. Capital of Scotland (9)
6. _ _ _ _ _ _ _ penguins are the largest birds of their kind (7)
7. Tall tree (3)
8. Group of singers (5)
9. Pale powder left after burning (3)
10. Frozen drips (7)
12. Plane trips (7)

DOWN

1. Southern _ _ _ _ _ _ _ _ seals are named for their great size and trunk-like nose (8)
2. Sprite, goblin (3)
3. Digging a tunnel, or underground home (9)
4. Less common (5)
5. Not dangerous (8)
8. Cold feeling in the air (5)
11. Ignited (3)

ACROSS

1. The Big Bad Wolf huffs and _ _ _ _ _ (5)

4. Big, hairy spider with striped legs (9)

6. Rider, commuter (9)

7. Gymnastic move in which you go head over heels sideways (9)

10. Venomous, black Australian spider with a scarlet stripe (7)

DOWN

1. Capital of France (5)

2. Australian _ _ _ _ _ _ - _ _ _ spiders are the world's deadliest (6-3)

3. Pricked painfully (5)

4. Subject (5)

5. On the 1st of which month do people play tricks on each other? (5)

8. Hang out to dry (3)

9. Large deer (3)

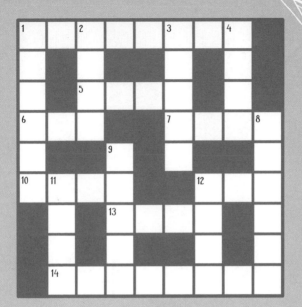

ACROSS

1. Grabs (8)
5. Den, hideout (4)
6. Showed the way (3)
7. Create (4)
10. Wound made by teeth (4)
12. A beret, for example (3)
13. Big mound of sand (4)
14. _____ spiders lie in wait in burrows with lids (8)

DOWN

1. Giant spider encountered by Frodo and Sam in *The Lord of the Rings* (6)
2. ____ *Lang Syne* is sung at New Year (4)
3. Damages (5)
4. Fine substance from which spiders make their webs (4)
8. One or the other (6)
9. Word for TV, radio, newspapers, and so on (5)
11. "___'_ it a lovely day?" (4)
12. Role model, idol (4)

ACROSS

1. Which creature beats a hare in a race, in a fable by Aesop? (8)
4. "Once _ _ _ _ a time…" (4)
6. America's largest state (6)
8. The _ _ _ _ _ _ Bunny leaves gifts of chocolate eggs (6)
10. US state (4)
11. Capital of Belgium (8)

DOWN

1. Bambi's rabbit friend (7)
2. Someone who pays rent (6)
3. Takes little drinks (4)
5. Rabbits love these orange vegetables (7)
7. Some answers go down, some go _ _ _ _ _ _ (6)
9. Old wound (4)

ACROSS

1. It rises from a kettle (5)
4. United _ _ _ _ Emirates (4)
6. _ _ _ _ _ Rabbit and his friends are always raiding Mr McGregor's garden (5)
7. Cover, enfold (4)
9. Leaps (4)
11. Alice followed the _ _ _ _ _ Rabbit down a hole to Wonderland (5)
13. Large, wild rabbit relative (4)
14. The Sun _ _ _ _ _ every morning (5)

DOWN

1. Brilliant, amazing (5)
2. Feed upon (3)
3. Alice met the _ _ _ _ _ Hare at the Mad Hatter's Tea Party (5)
5. _ _ _ _ Bunny, famous cartoon rabbit (4)
7. Clean yourself (4)
8. Strength, capability (5)
10. Push down, squeeze (5)
12. Belonging to it (3)

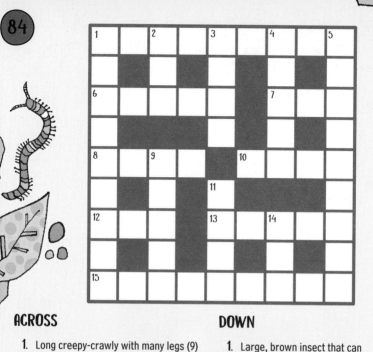

ACROSS

1. Long creepy-crawly with many legs (9)
6. Chop, slice (3, 2)
7. Stick for playing pool or snooker (3)
8. Danger (4)
10. Slimy garden pest (4)
12. Also known as (1.1.1.)
13. Stroll (5)
15. October 31st (9)

DOWN

1. Large, brown insect that can be a household pest (9)
2. "Last but _ _ _ least" (3)
3. Spotting game (1-3)
4. Succeed, flourish (5)
5. Having leaves all year round (9)
9. Shelled garden creature (5)
11. Stuffed tortilla (4)
14. Striped, flying insect (3)

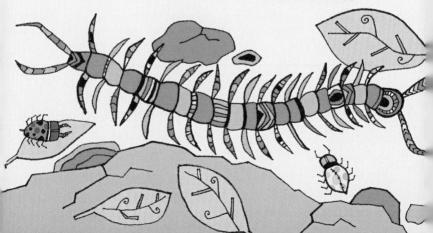

ACROSS

1. Long creepy-crawly with many, *many* legs (9)
6. Expected (3)
7. Move quietly (5)
8. Sore (4)
9. Having lots to do (4)
12. Young insect that looks very different from its adult form (5)
14. Flying saucer (1.1.1.)
16. Little bug that rolls up into a ball (9)

DOWN

1. Wet soil (3)
2. Bloodsucking worm (5)
3. Move slowly forward (4)
4. The first woman in the Bible (3)
5. Hollow (5)
8. Let happen (5)
10. Native Australian name of Ayer's Rock (5)
11. Pellets of frozen rain (4)
13. ___ de Janeiro, Brazilian city (3)
15. How many horns does a unicorn have? (3)

ACROSS

1. Huge, snapping reptile (9)
5. The 1 across has the world's
   _ _ _ _ _ _ _ _ _ bite (9)
7. Bulge, swelling (4)
9. Biting, hopping insect (4)
11. Sad (9)
13. Unlike its larger, brown relative, this North American wild animal can climb trees (5, 4)

DOWN

1. Fortresses (7)
2. Paddle for a boat (3)
3. Pig noise (4)
4. Perfect (5)
6. Advertisement for a movie (7)
8. Heroine of *The Sound of Music* (5)
10. Captain _ _ _ _ was pursued by a ticking 1 across (4)
12. Enemy (3)

ACROSS

1. Member of the crocodile family (9)
6. Very annoyed (5)
7. What does the symbol "&" mean? (3)
8. Big, fierce goblins in the books of J.R.R. Tolkien (4)
10. In which continent is China? (4)
12. Performing pair (3)
13. Marsh (5)
15. Jolliest (8)

DOWN

1. This South American swimming snake is the biggest in the world (8)
2. Sawn-off section of a tree (3)
3. Slang for "men" (4)
4. "Crocodile _ _ _ _ _" are false emotions (5)
5. It's rolled out for VIPs (3, 6)
9. Shut (5)
11. Operator (4)
14. Wonder (3)

ACROSS

1. Obtain (3)
3. _ _ _ _ _ frogs are so named because they are see-through (5)
6. Creature that lives both on land and in water (9)
7. Throw (4)
9. Fruit (4)
12. Large, winged insect of ponds and lakes (9)
14. June, for example (5)
15. Bind (3)

DOWN

1. Allow, permit (5)
2. Spinning toy (3)
3. Small pieces of stone (4)
4. Opposite of dead (5)
5. Male child (3)
8. Frog eggs (5)
10. Rolls _ _ _ _ _, luxury car (5)
11. This one as well as that one (4)
12. Faint, gloomy (3)
13. Plump (3)

89

ACROSS

1. Famous TV and movie frog (6)
5. Female singer below soprano (4)
6. Moved around to music (6)
9. Small pool, especially in a garden (4)
11. Frog parts eaten in France (4)
12. Twice ten (6)
15. Blue-green shade (4)
16. UK capital (6)

DOWN

1. Child (3)
2. ___ Weasley, Harry Potter's best friend (3)
3. Baby frog with a tail (7)
4. Warty, frog-like creature (4)
7. Dull pain (4)
8. High-quality glass (7)
10. Long-tailed amphibian (4)
11. Jump (4)
13. Move head up and down (3)
14. Currency of Japan (3)

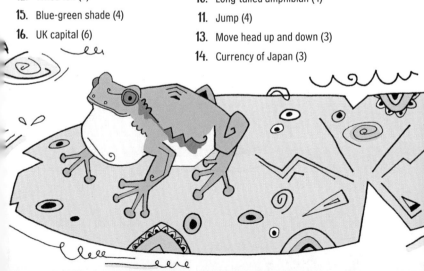

ACROSS

2. Shorten (4)
4. Large river rodent with a paddle-like tail (6)
6. Big, frizzy hairstyle (4)
7. Spiny North American mammal (9)
9. Side (4)
10. Rocky, rough (6)
11. 5 acrosses build them in rivers (4)

DOWN

1. Release (3, 2)
2. Capturing (8)
3. Huge Canadian deer with massive antlers (5)
5. Coupons (8)
7. Beg, implore (5)
8. More pleasant (5)

ACROSS

1. Bear-like Canadian animal that gave its name to the *X-Men* character played by Hugh Jackman (9)
5. Canada's flag is _ _ _ and white (3)
6. Liquid refreshment (5)
8. _ _ _ _ tea is drunk in summer (4)
9. Be concerned (4)
12. Large farm bird (5)
14. French for "street" (3)
15. Arctic rodents mistakenly believed to jump off cliffs in large packs (8)

DOWN

1. Striving (7)
2. A beaver's house, built of branches (5)
3. Tips (4)
4. French for "no" (3)
7. Guardians (7)
10. It protects a cook's clothes (5)
11. Bacterium (4)
13. Liquid grease (3)

92

ACROSS

1. Small, orange fish often kept as a pet (8)
5. Fierce river fish (4)
6. Spring, bound (4)
7. Questions (4)
10. Common lake fish (4)
13. Round, glass fish tank (4)
14. Opposite of odd (4)
15. Answer to a problem (8)

DOWN

1. Strong-tasting onion-like vegetable (6)
2. Fall slowly in drops (4)
3. Thought (4)
4. The _ _ _ _, angry green superhero (4)
5. Set of two (4)
8. In the near future (4)
9. Popular fish with pink meat (6)
11. Goals (4)
12. Skin, rind (4)
13. Most good (4)

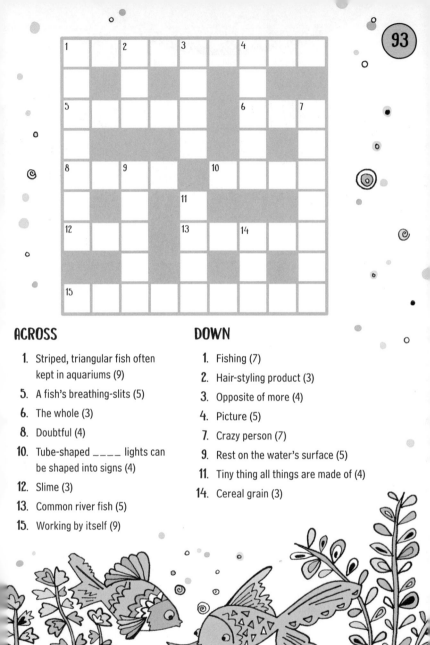

ACROSS

1. Striped, triangular fish often kept in aquariums (9)
5. A fish's breathing-slits (5)
6. The whole (3)
8. Doubtful (4)
10. Tube-shaped _ _ _ _ lights can be shaped into signs (4)
12. Slime (3)
13. Common river fish (5)
15. Working by itself (9)

DOWN

1. Fishing (7)
2. Hair-styling product (3)
3. Opposite of more (4)
4. Picture (5)
7. Crazy person (7)
9. Rest on the water's surface (5)
11. Tiny thing all things are made of (4)
14. Cereal grain (3)

ACROSS

1. _ _ _ _ _ _ monkeys are named for their bellowing cries (6)
5. If a door is _ _ _ _, it's slightly open (4)
6. Mexican animal with a jointed, leathery shell (9)
9. Four-sided shape (9)
12. You hit it with a hammer (4)
13. Dry, waterless (4)
14. Fashion, craze (3)

DOWN

1. _ _ _-_ _ _ balloons float in the sky (3-3)
2. Impulse (4)
3. Food allowance, as in wartime (6)
4. You kick it around (4)
7. Be present (6)
8. Unlocked (6)
10. At any time (4)
11. Ball sport with a long club (4)

ACROSS

1. Slender Latin American crocodile (6)
4. He was old, and had a farm (9)
6. Tiny Mexican dog (9)
9. "The cookies were left out so we helped _____" (9)
11. _ _ _ _ _ _ monkeys are named for their long, spindly arms, and their ability to dangle by their tails (6)

DOWN

1. Prickly desert plants (5)
2. Japanese comics (5)
3. Zero points (3)
4. Overly manly, cocky, aggressive (5)
5. Portrays, sketches (5)
7. Capsize, turn upside-down (5)
8. Hang in the air like a hummingbird (5)
10. Captain Kirk commanded the _ _ _ Enterprise (1.1.1.)

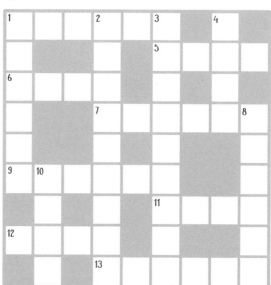

ACROSS

1. Rain cover, or top layer of rainforest (6)
5. "Beauty is ＿ ＿ ＿ ＿ skin-deep" (4)
6. Ancient Central American people (4)
7. 5×3×3×2 (6)
9. Monkey-like animals from Madagascar (6)
11. One of two siblings born together (4)
12. Permit to stay in a foreign country (4)
13. Cared back to health (6)

DOWN

1. Metal disc in a drum kit (6)
2. Red-haired ape (9)
3. Child (9)
4. Level, even (4)
8. Made a tired sound (6)
10. Wicked, malicious (4)

ACROSS

1. Quivered (8)
5. Say, pronounce (5)
6. Very slow-moving rainforest animal that lives mainly upside-down (5)
8. Musical symbols (5)
10. A secret _ _ _ _ _ is a spy (5)
11. The Latin American giant _ _ _ _ _ _ _ _ laps up little insects with its long, sticky tongue (8)

DOWN

1. Rainforest bird with a huge, brightly-patterned beak (6)
2. Amuse (9)
3. A jail has these (4)
4. Pleasure (9)
7. One who kills animals for food or sport (6)
9. Rescue (4)

ACROSS

1. Small, swift African antelopes (8)
6. Father's brother (5)
8. You have a big one on each foot (3)
9. Catch sight of, notice (4)
11. Automobiles (4)
14. Top, cover (3)
15. East African country (5)
18. High-jumping African antelope (9)

DOWN

1. Wildebeest (strange spelling) (3)
2. ___ Efron, US actor and singer (3)
3. Fibs (4)
4. More, surplus (5)
5. Stories of the day (4)
7. Short sleep (3)
9. Gives away for money (5)
10. Command (5)
12. Beam (3)
13. It covers your body (4)
16. Pen tip (3)
17. Noah's boat (3)

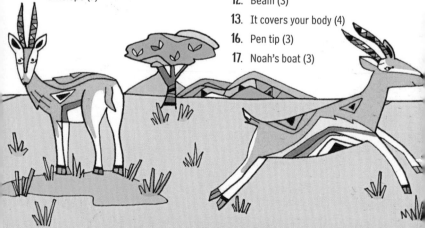

ACROSS

1. Song collection (5)
4. "Rub-a-dub-dub, three men in a _ _ _" (3)
6. Gone wild, full of weeds (9)
7. Green nut (9)
8. Africa is the second-largest _ _ _ _ _ _ _ _ (9)
10. British Special Forces unit (1.1.1.)
11. Cruel (5)

DOWN

1. A long time _ _ _ is far in the past (3)
2. "Count your _ _ _ _ _ _ _ _" means "Consider yourself lucky" (9)
3. Seasonal movement of animals, often to breed or find food (9)
4. What Hiccup names his dragon in *How To Train Your Dragon* (9)
5. Antelope that shares its name with a hand-drum (5)
7. Chooses (5)
9. A doll or ball, for example (3)

ACROSS

1. Umbrella-like sea creature (9)
6. You wear this on the beach to protect your skin (9)
8. Where a bird lays its eggs (4)
9. Untamed (4)
13. Long-snouted little ocean creatures with curling tails (9)
14. (see 13 down)

DOWN

1. Leader of the Argonauts (5)
2. Countryside painting (9)
3. Sound of disgust (4)
4. Short for "I have" (3)
5. Attila the ___, ancient warrior-chief (3)
7. Snake-like fish (3)
10. Matter, concern (5)
11. Sprint (4)
12. Horseback sport (4)
13. (with 14 across) Flower-like ocean creatures (3,

ACROSS

1. Five-armed sea creature (8)
7. Adult male (3)
8. Swells of the sea (5)
9. Friendly snowman in *Frozen* (4)
10. Whispered sound to get attention (4)
12. Conversations (5)
13. Nipped (3)
14. Used their ears (8)

DOWN

2. The snaking limbs of squid or jellyfish (9)
3. Lines (4)
4. Unseen (9)
5. Pause, dither (8)
6. The _____ jellyfish can live forever (if nothing eats it...) (8)
11. Small island (4)

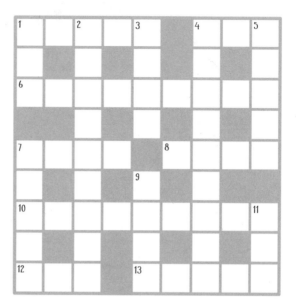

ACROSS

1. They go "quack!" (5)
4. Soft animal hair (3)
6. River rodent like a chubby rat (5, 4)
7. Animal hunted by another (4)
8. Chooses (4)
10. Blue-green shade (9)
12. Short for Sally (3)
13. Long-tailed river animal (5)

DOWN

1. Moisture that forms on the ground (3)
2. Important church with a bishop (9)
3. Organize (4)
4. Track, impression (9)
5. Tall riverside grasses (5)
7. Trails (5)
9. Martial art (4)
11. Organ of hearing (3)

ACROSS

1. Duck with a glossy, green head (7)
5. "I eat neither meat ___ fish" (3)
6. Male duck (5)
8. Is in debt to (4)
9. Command for a horse to slow (4)
12. Big, white water birds (5)
14. Spoken-word music style (3)
15. Cost (7)

DOWN

1. Common little fish in rivers and streams (9)
2. Big (5)
3. Short for Andrew (4)
4. Genetic code (1.1.1.)
7. Instance, illustration (7)
10. Tall river bird that patiently stalks fish (5)
11. Letters at the end of an invitation (1.1.1.1.)
13. Gobbled up (3)

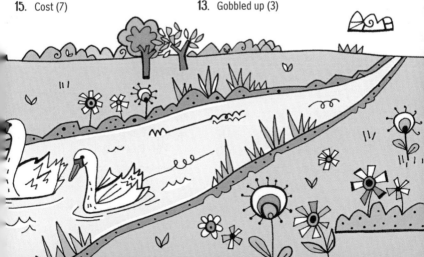

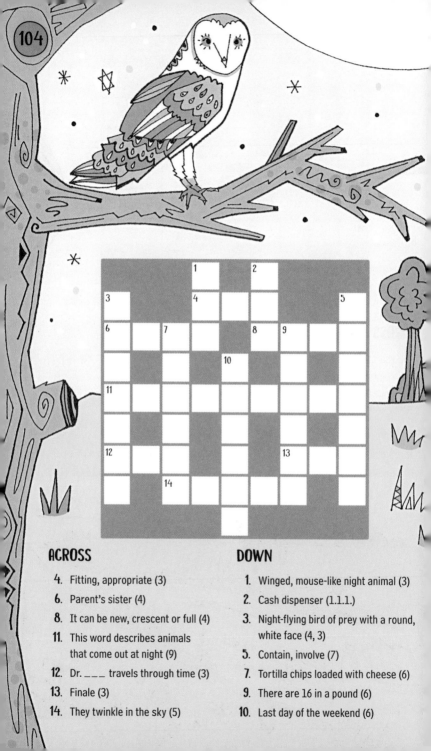

ACROSS

4. Fitting, appropriate (3)
6. Parent's sister (4)
8. It can be new, crescent or full (4)
11. This word describes animals that come out at night (9)
12. Dr. ___ travels through time (3)
13. Finale (3)
14. They twinkle in the sky (5)

DOWN

1. Winged, mouse-like night animal (3)
2. Cash dispenser (1.1.1.)
3. Night-flying bird of prey with a round, white face (4, 3)
5. Contain, involve (7)
7. Tortilla chips loaded with cheese (6)
9. There are 16 in a pound (6)
10. Last day of the weekend (6)

ACROSS

1. Small, prickly animal that rolls up into a ball when frightened (8)
5. Night-flying relatives of butterflies (5)
6. Sprite, pixie (3)
8. Jealousy (4)
10. Unbiased (4)
12. How many sides does a hexagon have? (3)
13. Indifferent, detached (5)
15. Improbable (8)

DOWN

1. They're used to drive in nails (7)
2. Small spot (3)
3. Uncomplicated (4)
4. High-class musical (5)
7. Insect that glows in the dark (7)
9. Female fox (5)
11. Cab (4)
14. The first odd number (3)

ACROSS

1. Sea fish with a striped, blue-green back (8)
5. Speedy sea fish with a long, sharp nose (9)
7. Dogs love to chase them (4)
10. Canvas sheet that catches the wind (4)
12. Long, fierce fish of tropical seas (9)
13. Depend (4)
14. Loan, allow someone to use (4)

DOWN

1. Pop or jazz, for example (5)
2. Lara _ _ _ _ _, raider of tombs (5)
3. Simple boats (5)
4. Short for Lesley (3)
6. Another name for the Netherlands (7)
8. Informed, in the know (5)
9. Fine mist (5)
11. Entertain, tickle (5)

ACROSS

1. What's the fishy last name of Tintin's sea captain friend? (7)

6. (with 8 across) Flatfish named for a citrus fruit (5, 4)

7. "Sing a song of sixpence, a pocketful of ___" (3)

8. (see 6 across)

10. Famous shark movie (4)

12. Noise, racket (3)

13. Japan's capital (5)

15. Small fish crammed into tins (7)

DOWN

1. Slope, cliff (8)

2. Not bright (3)

3. Possesses (4)

4. North and South _____, Asian nations (5)

5. Beach (8)

9. Connections (5)

11. Commotion, fuss (4)

14. Fancy Japanese carp (3)

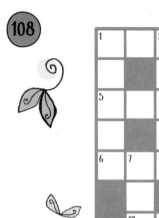

ACROSS

1. Fat, fuzzy, flying insect (9)
5. Daddy _ _ _ _ _ _ _ _, bug with thin, spindly limbs (8)
6. Wiggly soil creature (4)
9. Little green Jedi master (4)
12. Dusk; also a series of vampire romance novels (8)
13. TV host (9)

DOWN

1. Beneath (5)
2. Big country house (5)
3. Foe (5)
4. Became less difficult (5)
7. Opposite of inner (5)
8. "…with silver bells and cockleshells and pretty _ _ _ _ _ all in a row" (5)
10. If you should, then you _ _ _ _ _ to (5)
11. Dramatic performer (5)

ACROSS

1. Praying _ _ _ _ _ _, large green insect sometimes kept as a pet (6)
5. Corn or sugarcane, for example (4)
6. A caterpillar turns into one (9)
9. Lively (9)
12. Tiny, spider-like bug (4)
13. Struts of a bicycle wheel (6)

DOWN

1. Little toy glass ball (6)
2. Just after (4)
3. Rare, in short supply (6)
4. Dirt (4)
7. "Two's company, _ _ _ _ _'_ a crowd" (6)
8. Pleasure boats with a tricky spelling (6)
10. Hard covering on your fingertip (4)
11. Bloodsucking 12 across (4)

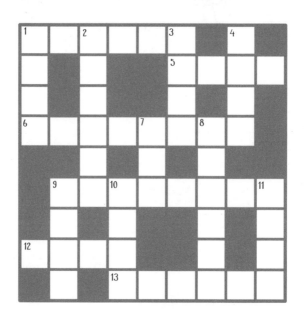

ACROSS

1. Super-smart person (6)
5. Use your eyes (4)
6. Chuckling, mirth (8)
9. They cover a bird's body (8)
12. Walk through water (4)
13. Immediately (2, 4)

DOWN

1. Common seabird (4)
2. Everything in the world that hasn't been made by people (6)
3. Cut, narrow opening (4)
4. Fly very high (4)
7. Opposite of cold (3)
8. 3+4+5−1 (6)
9. Move wings up and down (4)
10. Region (4)
11. Rescue (4)

ACROSS

1. Black-and-white seabirds with brightly-striped bills (7)
4. Unfastens, slackens (7)
8. The part of your life before you become an adult (9)
9. Letters sent overseas (7)
11. Things you wear (7)

DOWN

1. Large seabird with a huge beak (7)
2. Southernmost mainland state of the USA (7)
3. One of a community of religious "sisters" (3)
5. Someone older than you; also a tree (5)
6. Belly (7)
7. A duck _____ with its feet to swim (7)
10. Unwell (3)

ACROSS

1. Season following winter (6)
5. The chicken crossed it (4)
6. Hasty, careless (4)
8. "Don't count your chickens before they're _ _ _ _ _ _ _" (7)
10. Colonel _ _ _ _ _ _ _ founded KFC (7)
13. Yellow of an egg (4)
14. Female chickens (4)
15. Large farm bird (6)

DOWN

1. Swaggers (6)
2. Hurry (4)
3. _ _ _ _ _ _ _ stores sell mainly food (7)
4. Opposite of wild (4)
7. Most difficult (7)
9. Floppy-eared horse-like animal (6)
11. Old (4)
12. Leave in water (4)

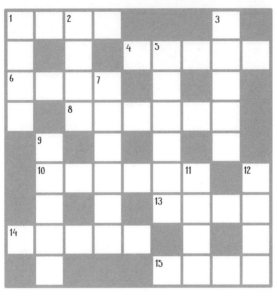

ACROSS

1. Hit with a beak (4)
4. Points total (5)
6. Make a noise like a rooster (4)
8. How much different things cost (6)
10. Baby toy (6)
13. Noble rank (4)
14. Fret (5)
15. Display (4)

DOWN

1. Walk back and forth (4)
2. Chicken run (4)
3. It's green and grows everywhere (5)
5. Laugh like a witch (6)
7. Author (6)
9. What a witch rides (5)
11. Every (4)
12. Opposite of fast (4)

114

ACROSS

1. Nostril on a whale or dolphin's head (8)
5. America (1.1.1.)
6. Velocity (5)
9. Cases, holdalls (4)
10. Hand out cards for a game (4)
12. Thick, sticky stuff oozing from trees (5)
14. What doctors make you say when they look in your mouth (3)
15. Tiny, drifting sea creatures eaten in vast quantities by whales (8)

DOWN

1. Whale fat (7)
2. Citrus fruits (7)
3. A firefighter uses one (4)
4. Old-fashioned word for "before" (3)
7. Classy and graceful (7)
8. Playful whale relative (7)
11. Short for anonymous (4)
13. Extra-sensory perception (1.1.1.)

ACROSS

1. Whales aren't fish, but _ _ _ _ _ _ _ (7)
5. Poem (3)
7. The Rock's real name is Dwayne _ _ _ _ _ _ _ (7)
8. Notice (4)
10. Having to do with the mouth (4)
12. Large, flexible fin (7)
14. Snip, sever (3)
15. Slim (7)

DOWN

1. Grand, awe-inspiring (8)
2. Miles per hour (1.1.1.)
3. As well (4)
4. Dolphins use a kind of _ _ _ _ _ to sense their surroundings (5)
6. Pioneer, trailblazer (8)
9. Presents (5)
11. Plunge (4)
13. Group of whales or dolphins (3)

ACROSS

1. Dogs bark, sheep _ _ _ _ _ (5)
4. Loft (5)
7. Change, adjust (5)
8. Sheep-like farm animal with horns and a beard (4)
9. Young sheep (4)
11. Star sign of the Ram (5)
13. Remove a sheep's wool (5)
14. Belonging to you (5)

DOWN

1. Sheep noise (3)
2. Way in (8)
3. Open-topped pie (4)
5. Italian coffee and cream dessert (8)
6. Hair-grooming tool (4)
8. Courage (4)
10. She had a little 9 across (4)
12. Distress signal (1.1.1.)

ACROSS

1. Herd of sheep (5)

4. Ice-conjuring princess in *Frozen* (4)

6. Female sheep (3)

7. Perils (7)

9. One of the fine hairs that protect your vision (7)

11. Short for *et cetera* (3)

12. Famous English boarding school for boys (4)

13. South America's longest mountain range (5)

DOWN

1. Coat of wool (6)

2. Well-behaved, dutiful (8)

3. Eager (4)

5. One who looks after sheep (8)

8. Quick bites (6)

10. 4 across's sister (4)

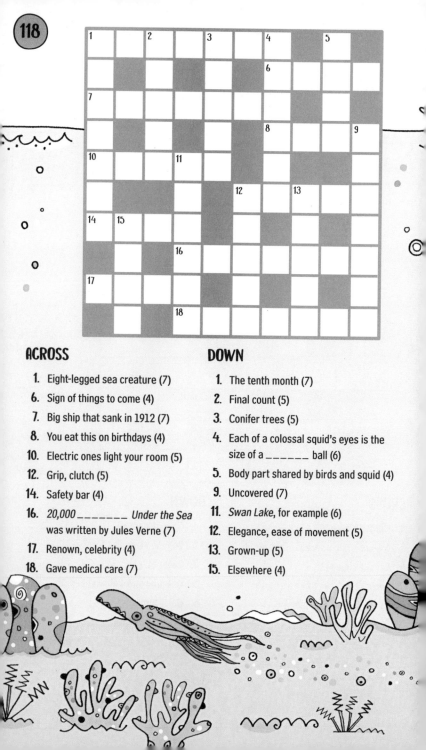

ACROSS

1. Eight-legged sea creature (7)
6. Sign of things to come (4)
7. Big ship that sank in 1912 (7)
8. You eat this on birthdays (4)
10. Electric ones light your room (5)
12. Grip, clutch (5)
14. Safety bar (4)
16. *20,000 _ _ _ _ _ _ _ Under the Sea* was written by Jules Verne (7)
17. Renown, celebrity (4)
18. Gave medical care (7)

DOWN

1. The tenth month (7)
2. Final count (5)
3. Conifer trees (5)
4. Each of a colossal squid's eyes is the size of a _ _ _ _ _ _ ball (6)
5. Body part shared by birds and squid (4)
9. Uncovered (7)
11. *Swan Lake*, for example (6)
12. Elegance, ease of movement (5)
13. Grown-up (5)
15. Elsewhere (4)

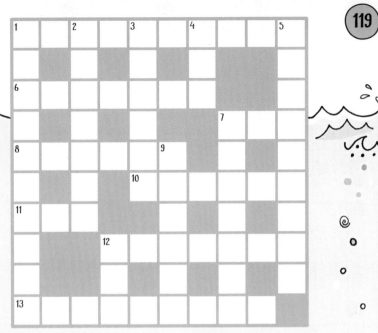

ACROSS

1. Broad, flat, squid-like sea creatures that squirt ink to confuse predators (10)
6. The Kraken is a legendary, giant, octopus-like sea _ _ _ _ _ _ _ (7)
7. How many limbs do squid have? (3)
8. Except that (6)
10. You swallow food through this (6)
11. Little electronic light (1.1.1.)
12. Short for "show business" (7)
13. Worn out (9)

DOWN

1. Blend in to your surroundings (10)
2. Intertwined, snarled up (7)
3. Most recent (6)
4. Distant (3)
5. Lull someone into a trance (9)
7. Difficulty, problems (7)
9. Darts forward (6)
12. The Mediterranean, for example (3)

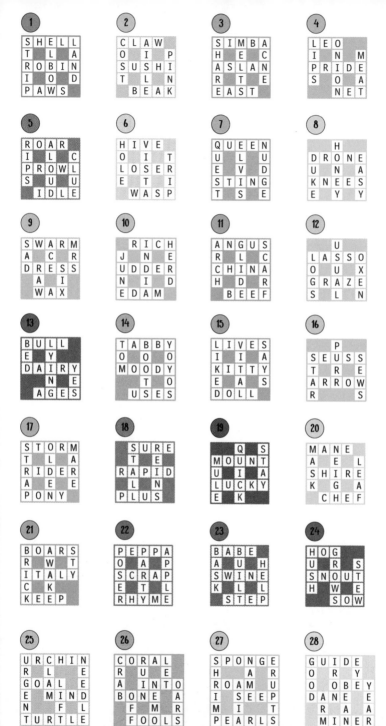

1
```
S H E L L
T   L   A
R O B I N
I   O   D
P A W S
```

2
```
C L A W
O   I   P
S U S H I
T   L   N
  B E A K
```

3
```
S I M B A
H   E   C
A S L A N
R   T   E
E A S T
```

4
```
L E O     M
I   N
P R I D E
S   O   A
    N E T
```

5
```
R O A R
I   L   C
P R O W L
S   U   U
  I D L E
```

6
```
H I V E
O   I   T
L O S E R
E   T   I
  W A S P
```

7
```
Q U E E N
U   L   U
E   V   D
S T I N G
T   S   E
```

8
```
      H
D R O N E
U   N   A
K N E E S
E   Y   Y
```

9
```
S W A R M
A   C   R
D R E S S
    A   I
W A X
```

10
```
  R I C H
J   N   E
U D D E R
N   I   D
E D A M
```

11
```
A N G U S
R   L   C
C H I N A
H   D   R
  B E E F
```

12
```
      U
L A S S O
O   U   X
G R A Z E
S   L   N
```

13
```
B U L L
E   Y
D A I R Y
    N   E
  A G E S
```

14
```
T A B B Y
O   O   O
M O O D Y
    T   O
  U S E S
```

15
```
L I V E S
I   I   A
K I T T Y
E   A   S
D O L L
```

16
```
    P
S E U S S
T   R   E
A R R O W
R       S
```

17
```
S T O R M
T   L   A
R I D E R
A   E   E
P O N Y
```

18
```
  S U R E
  T   E
R A P I D
  L   N
P L U S
```

19
```
  Q   S
M O U N T
U   I   A
L U C K Y
E   K
```

20
```
M A N E
A   E   L
S H I R E
K   G   A
  C H E F
```

21
```
B O A R S
R   W   T
I T A L Y
C   K
K E E P
```

22
```
P E P P A
O   A   P
S C R A P
E   T   L
R H Y M E
```

23
```
B A B E
A   U   H
S W I N E
K   L   L
  S T E P
```

24
```
H O G
U   R   S
S N O U T
H   W   E
    S O W
```

25
```
U R C H I N
R   L     E
G O A L   E
E   M I N D
N     F   L
T U R T L E
```

26
```
C O R A L
R   U   E
A   I N T O
B O N E   A
  F   M   R
  F O O L S
```

27
```
S P O N G E
H   A   R
R O A M   U
I   S E E P
M   I   T
P E A R L S
```

28
```
G U I D E
O   R   Y
O   O B E Y
D A N E   E
  R   A   A
  M I N E R
```

29
```
B A S S E T
E   E   H
H E E L   I
I     M O V E
N   N     F
D I N G O
```

30
```
T R I C K S
I   G   I
C A N I N E
K   O   D
L O R D S
E       E
```

31
```
B U R R O W
A   O   E
D A M P   A
G   E A R S
E       L   E
R E V E A L
```

32
```
F E R R E T
A   E   I
R   A S K S
M O L E   S
E     A   U
R A T T L E
```

33
```
    S H R E W
    K   O   A
M I S S   G
E   H E R E
E   O   O
K N E A D
```

34
```
M I C K E Y
A   O   A
Z   R A T S
E V E R   A
    E   E L
S T U A R T
```

35
```
C H E E S E
A     C   A
S I G H   S
U   N O T E
A   A   A L
L O W E R
```

36
```
    C L O C K
    I   L
    S A G A S
J E R R Y
    A   I
B L I N D
```

37
```
F O R G E T
A   A   R
S   T H O U
T R E E   N
E   A   K
N O B L E
```

38
```
I N D I A N
  U   S   E
S T U N   A
H   S T I R
O   E   T
T U S K S
```

39
```
J U M B O
A   O   U
I   S I T S
L A S T   O
N   E   L
  D U M B O
```

40
```
W A L K     I
I       I N N
G       W   C
O S T R I C H
P   H       A
E M U       R
N   S A N D
```

41
```
D O D O S
E   I   M
B I G B I R D
T   G   L   E
S P E C I A L
    R   N   A
    S O G G Y
```

42
```
A K E L A
L   N   C U B
P E T E R   R
A   E   O   A
C   R O B I N
A V E   A   C
    D U T C H
```

43
```
        I   B
    S I L V E R
    C   L   L
D E N   B O Y
    N   H   N
    R I D I N G
    C       T
```

44
```
S T U B B E D
E     L   I
R A C C O O N
E   H   O   E
A L A R M E D
L   R     A
M A M M O T H
```

45
```
S K U N K
O     H   G
B U F F A L O
B   I K   P
E N G L I S H
D   H     E
    T O W E R
```

46
```
      P R O D
    P E   R
D I S P L A Y
    L   T   G
M O N I T O R
    T   L   N
    S T E M
```

47
```
I G U A N A S
  E   L   I
S C A R I E R
  K   I   V
T O N G U E S
  A   H   N
D I C T A T E
```

48
```
F I R E A N T
L   E   R   E
Y U M M I E R
I   A   Z   M
N A I R O B I
G   N   N   T
  E S C A P E
```

49
```
P H A R A O H
A   P   U
N U R S E R Y
T   I   X   A
S O L D I E R
    I   T   D
G L A S S E S
```

50
```
K I N G     B
O       O G R E
N       R   A
G O L I A T H
    V   L   U
T A I L     G
    L   A B L E
```

51
```
B U B B L E S
A   A   E
G I B B O N S
G   O   N   T
I R O N A G E
E   N   R   R
R E S I D E
```

52
```
A D A M S
R   I   U   H
C A R I B O U
T   L   Z   N
I C E B E R G
C   S   R   R
    S N O W Y
```

53

```
O R C A S
P   E   T O W
P O L A R   A
O   S   A   L
S   I N N E R
E A U   G   U
    S E E K S
```

54

```
  C   V
L O C U S T S
  Y   L   H
P O T T E R Y
  T   U   E
M E E R K A T
    E   T
```

55

```
C A M E L
A   I   A I R
S I R E N   U
P   A   T   N
I   G R E E N
A Y E   R   E
N   S E N O R
```

56

```
      G A P S
S   R   O
L E O P A R D
I   W   C   A
P A N T H E R
    U   E   T
S P A R
```

57

```
    C   S   S
  B O B C A T
E   U   R   A
J A G U A R S
E   A   P   H
C A R E E R
T   S   D
```

58

```
P E T S
A   H   G A G
R A I S E   L
R   R   R   O
O   T U B E S
T R Y   I   S
    P L A Y
```

59

```
S Y R I A
A   I   C   T
H A M S T E R
A   A   U   E
R E B E C C A
A   I   O   T
    B O W L S
```

60

```
B A M B O O
O     A   W
O   W I N N I E
B E A T   E   M
O   K   T R I P
O L I V E S   I
    N   E   R
  G E N T L E
```

61

```
K U N G F U
I   E   L   D
C L A R I F Y
K   T   P O E M
S E E S   Z   A
  G R I Z Z L Y
  G   Z   I   O
  M E T E O R
```

62

```
C H E E T A H
O   A   E   Y
L   S N A K E
A R E   M   N
  A   I   M A C
  Z E B R A   A
  O   I   S   P
R O S E T T E
```

63

```
  S A F A R I
  O   I   N
J E W E L   J
A   E   M E N U
C O D E   R   R
K     M A R T Y
A   M   O
L A W Y E R
```

64

```
K A N G A R O O
O   I   X   V
A N G E L   E
L   H   E T N A
A C T S   R   S
  O   P O U C H
  O   O   M   E
P L A T Y P U S
```

65

```
C O W A R D S
U   O   O   U
C O M P O S E S
K   B   A   Y
O   A   L   D
O P T I C I A N
  E   L   V   E
W A L L A B Y
```

66

```
B U Z Z A R D
L   I   M   O K
O S P R E Y   E
S   P   N E T S
S E E D   L   T
O   D O L L A R
M A   R   E   E
  S C A N D A L
```

67

```
C O N D O R
O   A   M
M E R L I N
I   R   T O R E
C O O K   T   A
  W I R I N G
    T   C   L
  S E V E R E
```

68

```
C O B R A   H
O   O   D E A F
S E A   D   L
T     V E N O M
S T A I R   U
H   P   A I D
H I D E S   D
N   R E P L Y
```

69

```
J   M A M B A
O N E   O   L
Y   D U B L I N
F L U   A   O
U   S   S U B
L O A T H E   O
A   O   R I D
F A N G S   Y
```

70

```
G I R A F F E
L   I     L
O   A N N O Y S
R I F T   O   A
I   R   G R O W
A L I E N S   I
    C   A     N
  W A R T H O G
```

71

```
S A V A N N A H
T   O   E   P
A   W E A K E R
Y E S   T   H
U     S   A L I
P Y T H O N   N
  A   U   N   O
S P O T L E S S
```

72

```
S T I N G R A Y
A   N   R   L
F I N   E   O
E     M A N T A
R O B O T     F
  V   U   P I T
  E N   O     E
P R E D A T O R
```

73

```
B A S K I N G
L   E   R   I
O P T   K   F
O     T E E T H
D R O I D     E
  E   G   I L L
  S   E   C   L
  T O R P E D O
```

74

```
S Q U I R R E L
T   N   O     A
A   I N T E N D
G O T     F
      E     F O X
R I D D L E   R
E     O   C   A
D I R E C T L Y
```

75

```
A C O R N S
N   S   I
T   L   G R U B
L O O S E     R
E     H E D G E
R U B Y   A   E
    E     H   Z
  T W E L V E
```

76

```
P E A C O C K
E   H   A   D
R   M U M B A I
F R O M   B   G
U   W   K I N G
M A G P I E   I
E   L   L     N
  K I P L I N G
```

77

```
S I B E R I A N
N   A   U   S
A T L A S   A
P   O   T A P S
S L O T   G   H
  O   E R A S E
  V   X   I   R
S E N T E N C E
```

78

```
A L B A T R O S S
N   A   E   P   U
T O Y   S E A L S
A     T   L   P
R A K E   I S L E
C   R   P     N
T W I C E   A D D
I   L   G   H   S
C O L O S S A L
```

79

```
E D I N B U R G H
L   M   U   A   A
E M P E R O R   R
P     R   E L M
H   C H O I R   L
A S H   W       E
N   I C I C L E S
T   L   N   I   S
  F L I G H T S
```

80

```
    P U F F S
    A   U   T
T A R A N T U L A
O   I   N   N   P
P A S S E N G E R
I     L         I
C A R T W H E E L
  I   E   E     L
  R E D B A C K
```

81

```
S N A T C H E S
H   U   A   I
E   L A I R   L
L E D   M A K E
O     M   S   I
B I T E     H A T
  S   D U N E   H
  N   I   R   E
  T R A P D O O R
```

82

```
T O R T O I S E
H     E     I
U P O N     P   C
M     A L A S K A
P     N   C     R
E A S T E R     R
R   C     O H I O
    A     S     T
  B R U S S E L S
```

83

```
  S T E A M
  U   A   A R A B
  P E T E R     U
  E     C     G
W R A P   H O P S
A   O     O     R
S     W H I T E
H A R E   T   S
      R I S E S
```

84

```
C E N T I P E D E
O   O   S   X   V
C U T U P   C U E
K     Y   E   R
R I S K   S L U G
O   N   T       R
A K A   A M B L E
C   I   C   E   E
H A L L O W E E N
```

85

```
M I L L I P E D E
U   E   N V   M
D U E   C R E E P
    C   H     T
A C H Y   B U S Y
L     H   L
L A R V A   U F O
O   I   I   R N
W O O D L O U S E
```

86

```
C R O C O D I L E
A   A   I D
S T R O N G E S T
T     K A     R
L U M P   F L E A
E   A   H     I
S O R R O W F U L
    I   O   O E
B L A C K B E A R
```

87

```
A L L I G A T O R
N   O U   E   E
A N G R Y   A N D
C   S   R   C
O R C S   A S I A
N   L U       R
D U O   S W A M P
A   S E   W   E
  M E R R I E S T
```

88

```
G E T   G L A S S
R   O   R   L O
A M P H I B I A N
N     T V
T O S S   P E A R
    P   B     O
D R A G O N F L Y
I   W   T   A C
M O N T H   T I E
```

89

```
K E R M I T     T
I   O     A L T O
D A N C E D     A
    C   R   P O N D
    H   Y   O   E
L E G S   L   W
E     T W E N T Y
A Q U A   O   E
P     L O N D O N
```

90

```
    L       T R I M
B E A V E R     O
    T   O   A F R O
    G   U   P   S
P O R C U P I N E
L   H       I   I
E D G E   N     C
A   R U G G E D
D A M S       R
```

91

```
W O L V E R I N E
O   O   N     O
R E D   D R I N K
K   G S       E
I C E D   C A R E
N     G   P   P
G O O S E   R U E
  I   R   O   R
  L E M M I N G S
```

92

```
G O L D F I S H
A   R   D   U
R   P I K E   L
L E A P   A S K S
I   I     O   A
C A R P   B O W L
I   E V E N   M
M   E S       O
S O L U T I O N
```

93

```
A N G E L F I S H
N   E   E   M
G I L L S   A L L
L     S   G   U
I F F Y   N E O N
N   L   A     A
G O O   T R O U T
    A   O   A I
A U T O M A T I C
```

94

```
H O W L E R   B
O   H     A J A R
T   I     T   L
A R M A D I L L O
I       T   O   P
R E C T A N G L E
  V   E     O N
  E   N A I L   E
A R I D     F A D
```

95

```
    C A I M A N
    A     A   I
M A C D O N A L D
A   T     G   R
C H I H U A H U A
H     P     O W
O U R S E L V E S
S     N   E
  S P I D E R
```

96

```
C A N O P Y   F
Y     R   O N L Y
M A Y A   U   A
B     N I N E T Y
A     G   G   A
L E M U R S     W
  V   T   T W I N
V I S A   E
  L   N U R S E D
```

97

T	R	E	M	B	L	E	D	
O		N		A		N		
U	T	T	E	R		J		
C		E		S	L	O	T	H
A		R		Y		U		
N	O	T	E	S		M		N
	A		A	G	E	N	T	
	I		V		N		E	
A	N	T	E	A	T	E	R	

98

G	A	Z	E	L	L	E	S
N		A		I		X	N
U	N	C	L	E		T	O	E
	A		S		R		W
S	P	O	T		C	A	R	S
E		R		S			A
L	I	D		K	E	N	Y	A
L		E		I		I		R
S	P	R	I	N	G	B	O	K

99

A	L	B	U	M		T	U	B
G		L		I		O		O
O	V	E	R	G	R	O	W	N
			S		R		T	G
P	I	S	T	A	C	H	I	O
I		I		T		L		
C	O	N	T	I	N	E	N	T
K		G		O		S		O
S	A	S		N	A	S	T	Y

100

J	E	L	L	Y	F	I	S	H
A		A		U		V		U
S	U	N	S	C	R	E	E	N
O		D		K			E	
N	E	S	T		W	I	L	D
	C		P		S		A	
S	E	A	H	O	R	S	E	S
E		P		L		U		H
A	N	E	M	O	N	E	S	

101

	S	T	A	R	F	I	S	H
I		E		O		N		E
M	A	N		W	A	V	E	S
M		T		S		I		I
O	L	A	F		P	S	S	T
R		C		I		I		A
T	A	L	K	S		B	I	T
A		E		L		L		E
L	I	S	T	E	N	E	D	

102

D	U	C	K	S		F	U	R
E		A		O		O		E
W	A	T	E	R	V	O	L	E
		H		T		T		D
P	R	E	Y		O	P	T	S
A		D		J		R		
T	U	R	Q	U	O	I	S	E
H		A		D		N		A
S	A	L		O	T	T	E	R

103

M	A	L	L	A	R	D		
I		A		N		N		
N	O	R		D	R	A	K	E
N		G		Y				X
O	W	E	S		W	H	O	A
W			R		E			M
S	W	A	N	S		R	A	P
	T		V		O			L
E	X	P	E	N	S	E		

104

			B		A			
B		A	P	T		I		
A	U	N	T		M	O	O	N
R		A		S		U		C
N	O	C	T	U	R	N	A	L
O		H		N		C		U
W	H	O		D		E	N	D
L		S	T	A	R	S		E
				Y				

105

H	E	D	G	E	H	O	G
A		O		A		P	
M	O	T	H	S		E	L	F
M			Y		R		I
E	N	V	Y		F	A	I	R
R		I		T				E
S	I	X		A	L	O	O	F
	E		X		N			L
U	N	L	I	K	E	L	Y

106

M	A	C	K	E	R	E	L
U		R		A		E	
S	W	O	R	D	F	I	S	H
I		F		T				O
C	A	T	S		S	A	I	L
	W		P		M			L
B	A	R	R	A	C	U	D	A
	R		A		S			N
R	E	L	Y		L	E	N	D

107

H	A	D	D	O	C	K		
I		I		W		O	S	
L	E	M	O	N		R	Y	E
L			S		E		A	
S	O	L	E		J	A	W	S
I		I		S			H	
D	I	N		T	O	K	Y	O
E		K		I		O		R
	S	A	R	D	I	N	E	

108

B	U	M	B	L	E	B	E	E
E		A		N		A		
L	O	N	G	L	E	G	S	
O		O		M		E		
W	O	R	M		Y	O	D	A
U		A		U			U	C
T	W	I	L	I	G	H	T	
E		D		H			O	
P	R	E	S	E	N	T	F	R

109

```
M A N T I S   S
A   E     C R O P
R   X     A   I
B U T T E R F L Y
L   H   C     A
E N E R G E T I C
  A   E     I   H
M I T E     C   T
  L   S P O K E S
```

110

```
G E N I U S   S
U   A     L O O K
L   T     I   A
L A U G H T E R
    R   O   L
  F E A T H E R S
  L   R   V   A
W A D E     E   V
  P   A T O N C E
```

111

```
P U F F I N S
E   L     U
L O O S E N S   P
I   R   L   T   A
C H I L D H O O D
A   D   E   M   D
N   A I R M A I L
    L     C   E
  C L O T H E S
```

112

```
S P R I N G   T
T   U     R O A D
R A S H   O   M
U   H A T C H E D
T   R   E     O
S A N D E R S   N
  G E     Y O L K
H E N S     A   E
  D   T U R K E Y
```

113

```
P E C K     G
A   O   S C O R E
C R O W   A   A
E   P R I C E S
  B   I   K   S
R A T T L E   S
O   O   E A R L
W O R R Y   C   O
M     S H O W
```

114

```
B L O W H O L E
L   R   O     R
U S A   S P E E D
B   N   E   L   O
B A G S   D E A L
E   E   A   G   P
R E S I N   A H H
S     O   N   I
  P L A N K T O N
```

115

```
M A M M A L S
A   P   L   O D E
J O H N S O N   X
E     O   A   P
S I G N   O R A L
T   I   D     O
I   F L I P P E R
C U T   V   O   E
    S L E N D E R
```

116

```
B L E A T
A   N     A T T I C
A L T E R   I   O
  R   T   R   M
G O A T   L A M B
U   N   M   M
T   C   A R I E S
S H E A R   S   O
    Y O U R S
```

117

```
F L O C K
L   B   E L S A
E W E   E   H
E   D A N G E R S
C   I     P   N
E Y E L A S H   A
  N   N   E T C
E T O N     R   K
    A N D E S
```

118

```
O C T O P U S   B
C   O   I   O M E N
T I T A N I C   A
O   A   E   C A K E
B U L B S   E   X
E     A   G R A S P
R A I L   R   D   O
  W   L E A G U E S
F A M E   C   L   E
  Y   T R E A T E D
```

119

```
C U T T L E F I S H
A   A   A   A     Y
M O N S T E R     P
O   G   E     T E N
U N L E S S   R   O
F   E     T H R O A T
L E D     O     U   I
A     S H O W B I Z
G   E   T     L   E
E X H A U S T E D
```

First published in 2018 by Usborne Publishing Ltd, 83–85 Saffron Hill, London ECIN 8RT, England.
Copyright © 2018 Usborne Publishing Ltd. The name Usborne and the devices ♀♂ are Trade Marks of Usborne Publishing Ltd.